Cupcake

P9-DNG-879

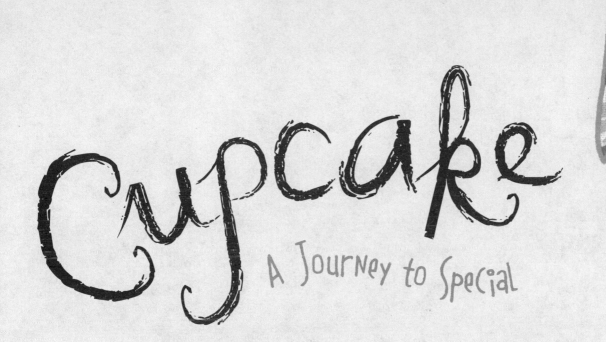

Cupcake

A Journey to Special

Charise Mericle Harper

SCHOLASTIC INC.
New York Toronto London Auckland
Sydney Mexico City New Delhi Hong Kong

For Henry, who loves all cupcakes,
and, because he likes to share,
Owen will help eat them up too!

No part of this publication may be reproduced, stored in a retrieval system, or transmitted in any form or by any means, electronic, mechanical, photocopying, recording, or otherwise, without written permission of the publisher. For information regarding permission, write to Hyperion Books for Children, an imprint of Disney Book Group, LLC, 114 Fifth Avenue, New York, NY 10011.

ISBN 978-0-545-45160-4

Text and illustrations copyright © 2010 by Charise Mericle Harper. All rights reserved. Published by Scholastic Inc., 557 Broadway, New York, NY 10012, by arrangement with Hyperion Books for Children, an imprint of Disney Book Group, LLC. SCHOLASTIC and associated logos are trademarks and/or registered trademarks of Scholastic Inc.

12 11 10 9 8 7 6 5 4 3 2 1   12 13 14 15 16 17/0

Printed in the U.S.A.   40

First Scholastic printing, January 2012

Book design by Teresa Kietlinski Dikun
Text set in Coffeedance and Journal
Art was drawn by hand and colored in Photoshop.

One day, in a big bowl, flour, sugar, eggs, milk, and baking powder were all mixed together.

And then, with just the right amount of
baking in a toasty hot oven . . .

. . . Cupcake was born.

After a special coat of icing, Vanilla Cupcake was creamy white, perfectly plain, and most certainly delicious.

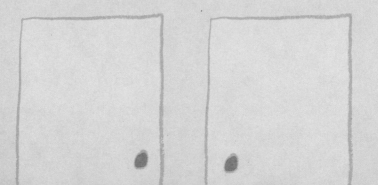

Being a friendly sort of cupcake, he quickly introduced himself to all his new brothers and sisters.

HI!

There was . . .

Happy-Face Cupcake

A smile a day makes the blues go away.

Pink Princess Cupcake

Charmed, I'm sure.

Chocolaty Chocolate Cupcake

It's Chocorific to meet you.

Cupcake felt special to be part of such a large
and colorful family.

Nobody picked me.
I'm too creamy white and plain!

But by the end of the day, Cupcake wasn't feeling
very special anymore. He was sitting on the plate
all alone.

A candle that was close by heard Cupcake crying and hopped over.

What's wrong?

I'M JUST Vanilla.
I'M NOT FANCY!
I'M just plain and white
and
ORDINARY.

"I know how you feel," said Candle, and then he told Cupcake all about *his* fancy brothers and sisters.

Let's see, there's . . .

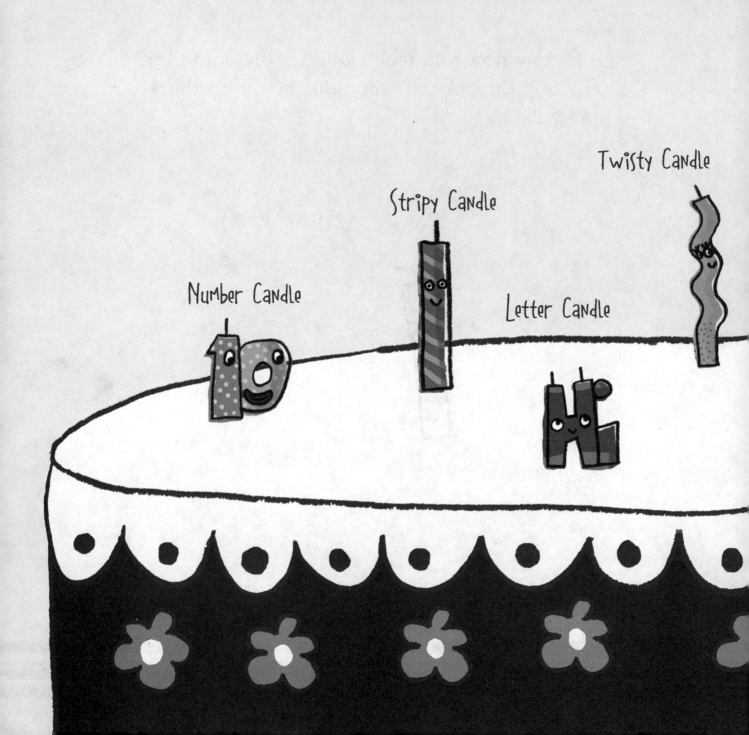

Number Candle

Stripy Candle

Letter Candle

Twisty Candle

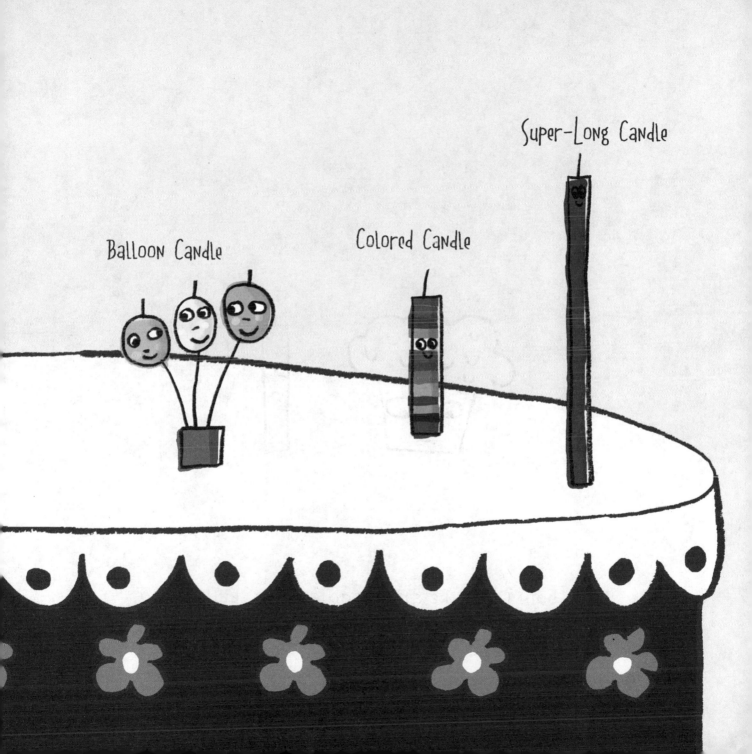

Balloon Candle

Colored Candle

Super-Long Candle

Now *both* Cupcake and Candle were feeling sad.

That is, until Candle had a big idea.

Hey, you JUST need a special topping.

"You're RIGHT!" said Cupcake. Candle hopped off to find the something special.

WOW!
He is so bright.

Candle had all sorts of suggestions.

Pickles!

"TOO salty!" said Cupcake.

Pancakes,

an egg,

PEAS.

And then . . .

A Squirrel!

Ughh! Too furry!

"I'm sorry," said Candle.
"I really thought we'd find something special."

Is he gone?

He's gone.

"Look!" said Candle. "What's that?"

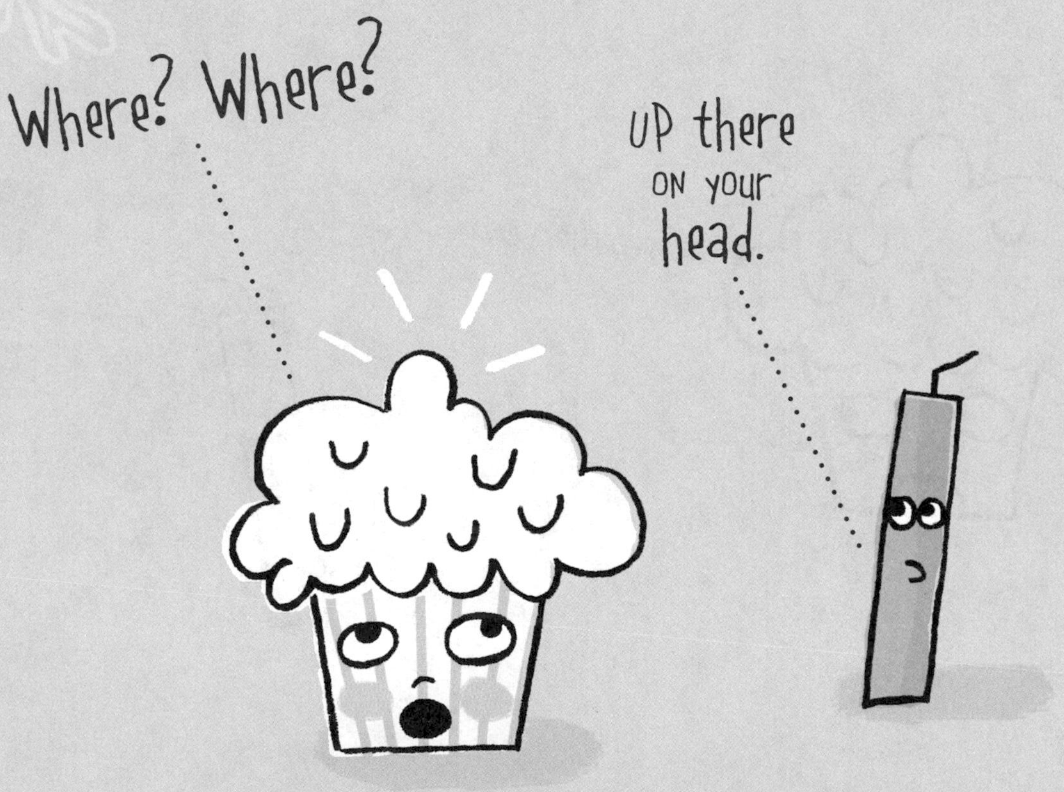

"There's something in here," said Candle.

"Wait! I've got it!" said Candle.

Recipe for Deliciously Plain VANILLA CUPCAKES

INGREDIENTS:

2 cups all-purpose flour
3 teaspoons baking powder
½ teaspoon salt
½ cup butter
1 ½ cups sugar
4 eggs, separated
1 cup 2% milk
1 ½ teaspoons vanilla

PREPARATION:

1 • Preheat oven until toasty (350°).

2 • Line cupcake pans with paper liners.

3 • Combine flour, baking powder, and salt, set aside.

4 • In new bowl combine butter, 1 cup of sugar, egg yolks, milk, vanilla, and a little bit of love.

5 • Now add dry ingredients to this mix.

6 • Mix at low speed for 2 minutes. Scrape bowl.

7 • Whip up remaining sugar with the egg whites, mixing at high speed until fluffy and smooth.

8 • Fold this into batter. It is going to be yummy!

9 • Fill liners one half to two thirds full of batter. Do not overfill.

10 • Bake 20 to 25 minutes or until toothpick inserted in centers comes out clean.

11 • Cool 10 minutes in pans, then remove and place on a wire rack to cool completely.

12 • Frost with Deliciously Plain Buttercream Frosting and ENJOY!

Deliciously Plain BUTTERCREAM FROSTING

INGREDIENTS:

½ cup butter, softened
4 cups powdered or
   confectioners' sugar
¼ teaspoon salt
4–5 tablespoons milk
2 teaspoons vanilla

PREPARATION:

1 • In large bowl, cream butter until very fluffy.

2 • Add part of the sugar and the salt and beat again.

3 • Continue adding sugar and milk in small batches, alternately, beating until very fluffy.

4 • Stir in vanilla.

5 • Frost your Deliciously Plain Cupcakes and eat! YUM.